AF231416

# Histories

by SUE LI

Arch Street Press
Bryn Mawr, PA · USA



First Arch Street Press edition December 2016

ARCH STREET PRESS, ARCH ST. PRESS
and colophon are registered trademarks of Arch Street Press.

For information about special discounts for bulk and nonprofit purchases, please contact Arch Street Press: sales@archstreetpress.org.

Cover design by idesign communications

Library of Congress Cataloging-in-Publication Data is available.

ISBN: 978-1-938798-16-0
ISBN: 978-1-938798-14-6 (e-book)

# Histories

If Dr. David Muller had emerged from his office five minutes earlier, he would have found me eagerly perusing the brochures on display in the Department of Medical Education at the Icahn School of Medicine at Mount Sinai, the very picture of an inquisitive doctor-to-be. Instead he caught me slouching in the waiting-room chair, idly scratching the nape of my neck while trying to discern the color of the carpet.

"Hi," I stammered, leaping to my feet. I introduced myself.

"Hello. I'm David."

I recalled his numerous titles. Dean for Medical Education. Professor and Systems Chair for Medical Education. Professor of Medicine. Founder of the Visiting Doctors Program. I had googled him so extensively that my Web browser automatically populated his name whenever I typed the letters "DA—" into the search bar. *David Muller, MD*. I followed him out of the waiting area and into his office, which boasted what an NPR correspondent once described as "[a] commanding view of the East River and East Harlem." A tall shelf crammed with books rested against one wall. We took seats at the conference table, and I tried to explain what I was doing in his office on a Monday afternoon.

"I was wondering if I could ask you what brought you to medicine?"

"Wow. What brought me to medicine? I think it was mostly happenstance." He explained that he had attended Johns Hopkins University. "Literally every guy in my dorm was premed—everyone. So I majored in premed." He gave a small, wistful smile. "It's kind of a disappointing story. It wasn't like, 'I love science and I want to change the world.' It just sort of happened."

I spoke with Muller in June of 2015, shortly after completing my first year of medical school. But the process that brought me to his office began many months before. With only a few weeks of medical school under my belt, I started questioning—in the brief interludes between classes and in the small hours of the night—whether medicine was right for me. My thoughts were a swarm of anatomical terms, blood supplies and innervations. My conversations, even with friends pursuing other careers, revolved around medicine. I found myself pushed to the limit, barely keeping afloat. New York City, once the subject of fantasies, quickly became the backdrop to my despair. *My biggest fear,* I wrote in a blog post, *is that one day I'll look back and realize that all I did during medical school was medicine.*

Have I made the wrong decision? About half of physicians would, if given the chance, choose a different profession. In a 2008 survey, a mere 6% of the 12,000 respondents described their morale as "positive." Essays on the matter, often written by physicians themselves, revealed widespread disillusionment due to stress, overwork, interpersonal conflict and a whole host of other factors. A physician-wellness presentation at my medical school, though well-intentioned, left me fearful of what lay ahead.

Doubtful of my own reasons for pursuing medicine, I decided to ask the people around me. I hoped that their stories would serve as a mooring post—perhaps remembering why we came to medical school would help us get through it. Above all, I wanted reassurance that I was neither the only one questioning nor the only one afraid.

In January of 2015, I ate dinner with a friend at an Indian restaurant in East Harlem. I told him that I was hoping to interview our classmates and faculty about what brought them to medicine. The words barely left my mouth when his eyes lit up.

"You have to interview Michael."

Michael, 28, was also a first-year medical student. All I knew about him was that he had taken some time off before medical school, for he looked a few years older—and many years wiser—than me. When we met, I was surprised by how deliberately he spoke. His words, unlike everything else in New York City, had no sense of urgency. When he was 24, Michael was working at an entry-level job, doing post-production work on television commercials. One day, he started seeing double.

"I would see two of things," Michael explained. "It's actually double vision. Can you cross your eyes?"

I gave it a try, staring at my index finger while bringing it toward my face. A few inches from my nose, I saw two blurry fingers, side by side.

"You know how things split apart?" Michael asked. "It was like that, but things were still in focus."

He wore an eye patch to prevent the double vision and put off seeing a doctor because work was busy. He simply thought that he was fatigued:

"Oh, it's just my eyes. I'm tired. I'm really tired of focusing, ha-ha," he joked. But the problem worsened, and he finally saw an ophthalmologist. An MRI revealed a chondrosarcoma—a slow-growing, non-aggressive tumor—in his skull base. He'd probably had it since birth.

"But at first I didn't know that. I just saw this big tumor in my head, pushing on my brain, wrapped around my carotid. What nerve was it pressing on, do you know?" I tried in vain to recall the anatomy that I had learned just a few months before. Seeing my hesitation, Michael answered for me:

"Sixth cranial nerve."

He had suffered from a partial palsy, an incapacitation of the nerve responsible for controlling the lateral rectus muscle of the eye, which allows the eyeball to turn outward. With a palsy, one eye turns but the other remains in place, and what would have converged into a single image splits into two.

According to Michael's doctor, there are only five cases of skull-base chondrosarcomas per year in the United States. As he learned more about his condition, Michael found himself drawn to biology, a subject that he thought he hated.

"I took AP biology in high school and it was awful. I don't think I knew—I mean, I had a hunch—that we were made of atoms. That's how unclear the class was." A few months after the diagnosis, Michael underwent a successful surgery to remove the tumor. Upon his recovery, he borrowed an anatomy book from his girlfriend at the time, who was studying to become a physician's assistant. He read through it—a feat that deeply impressed me given my Sisyphean struggle with the *Gray's Anatomy for Students* textbook—and wanted more. He left his job. While undergoing two months of radiation therapy at Massachusetts General Hospital, he squeezed in a few prerequisite courses for nursing school, under the impression that, for a philosophy and political-science major, medical school was out of reach.

"I didn't think that I could make it into medical school," Michael confessed.

His illness had left him anxious and emotionally vulnerable. He recalled his dad walking into his bedroom one day and asking, "Mike, why aren't you going to be a doctor?"

After much consideration, he decided to give it a try. "I was 99% sure I wanted to go to medical school," Michael said. "But if I was going to do it, I needed to be 100% sure."

"How did you become 100% sure?" I asked.

Medicine, in my mind, was so terrifyingly complex—how could anyone be absolutely committed, beyond a shred of doubt? Michael said that shadowing experiences had left a deep impression.

"There was something about seeing these doctors interact with their patients one-on-one that I identified with."

The physicians he encountered struck a delicate balance of expertise, humor and compassion.

"Before these experiences, being a doctor was a concept in my head that sounded good, but seeing them in action gave me role models I wanted to emulate."

It was enough to get him over the fence. He applied and was accepted to a one-year post-baccalaureate program at Bryn Mawr College. In the fall of 2013, nearly two years after his diagnosis, Michael applied to the Icahn School of Medicine at Mount Sinai.

"And now you're here."

"And now I'm here." Michael smiled. "It's been a ride."

I formally interviewed 15 students at Mount Sinai, while countless more spoke to me casually, off the record and in passing. What brought them to medicine? Like Michael, many students recounted experiences, chief among them shadowing, that led to the desire to become a doctor. But Sar's story stuck with me because, unlike the rest of us, he was the only one who had taken care of patients on his own. When I met him, he was one month away from completing his MD and headed to Emory for a residency in emergency medicine. He told me about the summer after his freshman year of college in which he worked for Dr. Rick Hodes, an American internist in Ethiopia who specialized in pediatric oncology, heart disease and spinal conditions. Sar was the only volunteer that summer. They worked in an 800-bed facility run by nuns; the patients were the destitute and dying. He was responsible for "daily minutiae"—taking kids for labs and refilling prescriptions. Then his mentor left for a 10-day speaking and fundraising tour in the United States.

"He said, 'Alright, Sar. Here's my list of patients. Here's when they're each getting chemo, here are the labs they're going to need. I trust you. If anything comes up, give me a call,'" Sar shared. "I was 19 at that point and thought, 'Holy shit, this is kind of crazy.'"

On the third day of Dr. Hodes's absence, Rufael, a 13-year-old with stomach cancer, refused to take his medicine. He and his mother had traveled a great distance from the countryside, where they farmed and tended goats, to reach the clinic in Addis Ababa. His mother believed that God would save her son from cancer. The boy wanted to be a priest—the most respected and well-educated of the people he knew. Every day, Rufael took around 80 pills, potassium supplements because his body was wasting potassium, and drugs for peptic ulcers.

"I can't eat anything because I'm taking so many pills," the boy said to Sar.

"Well, actually, those pills are keeping you alive right now. So if you stop taking them, it's going to be a big, big problem," Sar replied.

He told me that Rufael was a smart kid, very much a teenager and a little manipulative.

"He'd say, 'Oh, I'm not going to take my medicine unless you get me a candy bar.' So we would do that a few times."

When Sar spoke with Dr. Hodes on the phone that evening, Hodes gave him permission to let the boy take 40 pills instead. But Rufael still refused to take any pills at all.

"We spent a lot of time in silence," Sar said. "He liked doodling, so he would sit there and doodle, and I'd sit on the end of his bed. And he'd say, 'Alright, when are you leaving?' 'When you take your medicine.' And we'd be quiet for an hour, and he'd ask me again."

It was a 20-hour crisis. Well into the night, Rufael finally agreed to take 40 pills. "It was a very anticlimactic ending when he said, 'Fine, I guess.' I made him shake hands on it."

At last, Sar went home.

"I remember leaving exhausted at the end of the day. I don't know if I saved his life that day, but I definitely felt like I had helped him live to see another day, which was a very powerful feeling. It was my first time taking care of patients. I did it and thought, 'This is all I want to do.'"

Unlike Sar, I never had a moment of epiphany that sparked my interest in medicine, but there were plenty of times when being a doctor was the last thing that I wanted to do. My parents, who grew up in China, were both doctors. The best university in their province was a medical school; students picked their careers by applying to trade-specific institutions upon graduating from high school.

"We didn't think back and forth," my mother said, baffled by my desire to understand her and my father's motives. They had good test scores. They went to medical school. Three decades later, I can see why my parents are tempted to apply the same logic to me. I had good grades. I ought to go to medical school. Why waste the opportunity?

After my freshman year of college, I announced to my parents that I wanted to be an English major. They were, in short, furious. They implored me to switch to biology; medicine, in their opinion, was the only suitable career. Then my mother made me an offer: I could major in English, but had to go to medical school. It seemed the only option at the time, short of lying about my major. The following semester, I enrolled in Major English Poets, Introduction to Writing Fiction, a foundational biology course and Organic Chemistry. To my surprise, Chaucer was a welcome relief from arrow pushing, and arrow pushing a relief from Chaucer. On the long walk between the English Department and science laboratories, I wondered if I could marry the two or if I would have to decide, in the end, one way or another.

Josh's parents weren't at all like mine.

"I grew up in an atmosphere where education wasn't really valued," he said, a first-year student in the MD-PhD program at Mount Sinai. "I didn't turn in homework; I didn't study for anything. I didn't care about school at all. Nobody really cared about school."

His family wanted him to be a diligent worker and a task-seeker, not an academic, so Josh spent his days hard at work, delivering newspapers, stocking shelves at a grocery store and building houses. In his junior year of high school, he watched an episode of *House* that changed his idea of higher learning.

"There was a patient from an Amish or Mennonite family, who didn't want him to get a good education. But he was really interested in science. One of the characters identified with this patient and said, 'You know, we have a program here for students to come and do science.'"

Josh seemed bashful for a moment.

"It never even occurred to me that people, or students, would do research. And the very idea of someone being a scientist was so foreign to me."

An Internet search led Josh to Young Epidemiology Scholars—a scholarship competition in which students submitted original research, usually under the guidance of a mentor. But research scientists were scarce in his hometown, so he put together his own study investigating binge drinking in high-school students.

"Was that your first time doing research?" I asked.

"Oh, any at all! I had no idea what I was doing. But I wanted to do the competition and wanted to go to Washington, D.C. to get a scholarship. So I read five or six books on research methodology, about control groups that, you know, I'd never heard of before."

He knew that alcohol had a depressive effect on the immune system and thought maybe there was a connection between students drinking alcohol, falling ill and missing school. He surveyed a total of 700 students at his high school and at one 20 miles away. The liberal-arts college in his town owned a few back issues of *The Journal of the American Medical Association* and *The New England Journal of Medicine*, which Josh scoured for any studies pertaining to alcohol or the immune system. It was his first time doing a literature search. He taught himself statistics after buying a used book on eBay and learning Epi Info—a statistics program for epidemiology.

"The study was so poorly designed that I don't think any real conclusions could be drawn from it," Josh admitted. But the judges were impressed; Josh advanced to the regional finals for Young Epidemiology Scholars and was flown to Washington, D.C. to present his study. The keynote speaker, the president of the Institute of Medicine, mentioned the phrase "MD-PhD" during his remarks.

"I had never heard of this thing before," Josh told me.

He wanted to learn more. That year, he worked as an aide in a nursing home, which he claims was the best job he'd ever had: it left him with a desire to apply his love of science to improve patients' lives.

Josh's parents were opposed—"hostile," in his words—to the amount of education he wanted to pursue. They had not saved any money, so when Washington University in St. Louis accepted Josh, he supplemented his scholarship with loans. After graduating from college, he obtained a master's degree in History and Philosophy of Science from University College London and is expected to complete his MD-PhD in 2022.

"I'm very much a black sheep in my family."

While I could scarcely imagine spending eight years pursuing an MD-PhD, even four years of medical school—and many more of overnight shifts, beeping pagers and restless sleep—loomed large in my mind. The word "medicine" conjured visions of exhilaration, discovery and compassion, but also trauma, anxiety and grief. Fresh out of college, it was hard to commit to the former while accepting the latter—all the more difficult because I had little experience with either, and so my visions grew all the more foreboding as school began and the months flew by.

To my relief, I discovered that I was by no means the only person who had doubts about medicine. After completing my first year of medical school, I spoke with Dr. Basil Hanss, renal physiologist and former director of the Humanities and Medicine program, an early-acceptance program at Mount Sinai to which students apply during their sophomore year of college. It was through this that I had been admitted to medical school; it has since been renamed FlexMed and expanded to encompass students of all academic backgrounds.

According to Hanss, who has mentored countless students during his 20 years at Mount Sinai, doubt is a critical part of the process:

"My bias is that people who have never doubted are not thinking about it," he said. "I could be wrong. But my belief is that you've got to question it and, if you don't, you're not necessarily thinking through what you're doing. Medical school is not easy. I think it would be weird if a medical student didn't, at some time in those four years, say, 'What the hell am I doing to myself? Is it really worth doing this?'"

When I asked my classmates if they had doubts about medicine, some paused before saying no. Many more said yes.

"Today, I could walk out the door and be a teacher," said Janet, a first-year medical student. "I would probably enjoy it and could have it long-term. Why am I putting myself through this very, very difficult schooling process when I could have a schedule that would seem more sane?"

Her family, she said, would support her should she ever change her mind about medicine.

"I'm never stuck. If it ever comes to the point where I say, 'I don't want to be in medical school anymore—I don't really want to be a doctor'—fine. I'll drop out. That takes the pressure off. I never feel like decisions that I make are absolute."

The word "doctor" comes from the Latin word *docere*, which means "to teach." In college, I volunteered as a health educator in the city of New Haven, which involved leading 45-minute workshops for local teens on topics such as nutrition, substance abuse, intimate-partner violence, mental health, sexually transmitted infections (STIs) and contraception. I had joined the group on a whim, as a freshman eager to try something new, and it quickly became one of my favorite activities. I found teaching enjoyable rather than tedious, and each session left me invigorated no matter how late I had stayed up to prepare the night before. Questions asked in earnest ("You have to take birth control pills every day?" "Mountain Dew doesn't kill sperm?") both perplexed and inspired me to continue my efforts as an educator. What if, I wondered, I could have these conversations every day? Instead of referring teens to the nearest clinic, I wanted to be the one performing physical examinations and providing counseling. Becoming a doctor, I reasoned, would allow me to do just that. Perhaps there was a moment; perhaps there were a thousand. I had only told this story a handful of times and never once committed it to paper for fear that my words would fall short. What brought me to medicine was nothing more than a gym full of high-school students at 7 in the morning.

But what of Dean Muller, who said that his path to medicine was "mostly happenstance"? His "disappointing story" certainly had not prevented him from having a successful and fulfilling career. When Muller was a student, the top three reasons for pursuing medicine were money, love of science and desire to help people. In his opinion, those three reasons remain prominent today, but their relative importance has changed.

"My impressions are hugely skewed by being here at Mount Sinai. I think we are in an environment where money is not something people talk about much at all, so it's fallen down to number three. Also, the world has changed—if you really want to make big money, you go into another field. The science, I think, is still very potent. In my mind, it might be number two."

The students applying to medical school have changed, but science itself has also changed, less abstract and more clinically actionable today than when Muller was a medical student.

"And number one is this idea of becoming an important part of the social fabric. People know it's a bit clichéd to say, 'I want to help people,' even if they mean it.

But there's a sense of belonging, however you define it. I like to believe that, at this institution, it's the number-one thing people say."

According to Muller, the myriad motives that push someone toward medicine may become artificially distilled into a few familiar categories through the admissions process. Students who could have written a bolder essay may find themselves afraid to go out on a limb for fear that they will not be well received and their chance at medical school squandered. What one feels most passionately may not find its fullest expression on paper—or in an interview.

When I spoke to my classmate, Linda, she suggested that the idea of combining career and passion may be a contemporary one, open only to members of a high socioeconomic stratum.

"I read an article by Cal Newport," she said. "The gist was that this idea in America of finding your 'passion' and your 'calling' is false and too idealistic. Your calling in life is what you make of it. Find something you like that your skillset fits, and then it's the commitment that matters. I don't think medicine is my calling."

I was startled. Surely she had not written that in her application. I had assumed that everyone who worked in medicine considered it their calling, that anything less would result in crisis. But Linda's voice betrayed no sign of doubt.

"I like medicine enough," she offered, "and I think my personality fits it, and I'll just stick with it."

To be utterly devoted at all hours of the night is simply too much to expect, Linda explained, and moments will inevitably arise when being a doctor will feel more like work than passion. In other words, pursuing medicine is like being in a relationship.

"You go through phases," she concluded. "There are times when you feel intensely in love."

There are times when you hate each other's guts. The relationship lasts a lifetime; the trials are simply a part of the process.

The lounge in Aron Hall—a residential building for Mount Sinai students—was occupied, so Christian, a first-year medical student, suggested that we conduct the interview outdoors. Thirty seconds in, I was shivering, my penmanship reduced to that of a kindergartner, and I wondered if I had made a mistake. Christian did not seem to mind the springtime chill. Then again, he was wearing long sleeves.

"There was this one nagging thought that always bothered me," he said, "and that was the idea that when you grow up, some of your illusions fade away and the world becomes a harsher place. The world is so chaotic. Nature is indifferent and doesn't care if you're old or young or a child or loving or hateful. It'll kill anybody. I didn't see a fairness in that."

Christian often spoke in paragraphs and his tendency to gaze, unfocused, into the distance gave me the impression that I was privy to an inner monologue years in the making.

"I think ultimately people need purpose, whether it's told to them or they find it themselves."

But what was his purpose?

"I thought that in the short time we have on earth, everyone deserves a fighting chance to live the best life they can. I just wanted to add to that."

But he felt that many of his college classmates had been so focused on their acceptance to medical school that they lost sight of the bigger picture.

"I didn't want that to be the only defining quality of my life, that I went to medical school and became a doctor, and that's it."

Christian grew up in Jackson Heights, Queens. His parents emigrated from Latin America. He and his siblings were always taught to take care of each other, their house, their front yard, their street.

"You build your identity partly on your geography, your location. This is our block. This is our neighborhood."

When he saw younger kids fighting on the street, he would stop them, saying, "This doesn't belong to you. You can't do this here. This is a place of order and peace."

He lived in Jackson Heights his whole life before moving to attend Columbia University.

"It's the only thing you need to know about me. Who's Christian? That guy from Queens."

I imagined that if Christian were my patient, I would write in my notes: Christian, that guy from Queens. Then I wondered if that was precisely what I was doing—reducing people's lives to concise entries that could do no justice to the complexity of lived experience. Christian Pina, that guy from Queens, presents with acute anger at the indifference of society. I thought of Adam Gopnik's essay, "Word Magic," in which he writes, "*Histoire* in French means both 'history' and 'story,' in a way that 'history' in English doesn't quite… [lending itself to] the notion that histories are narratives we make up as much as chronicles we discern." In medicine, "history" is abbreviated Hx and is divided into further abbreviations—such as CC, HPI, PMH, PSH and more. But what story can be told through such bland elements as Chief Complaint, History of Present Illness, Past Medical History, Past Surgical History, Medications and Allergies? As one student put it, "There's more to life than medicine."

Like me, George was admitted to Mount Sinai through the Humanities and Medicine program, so I was surprised that he began our interview by describing his love of the sciences. Curious about the human body, he was excited to study anatomy, the first course in Mount Sinai's medical-school curriculum.

"The first day was jarring…. We unveiled the cadaver and freaked out. But as I was going through the class, I had all these existential moments where I would be dissecting a portion of the body and discovering how my own body was working, what made me able to move my arm up and down or my fingers back and forth. It was a journey into learning about the physicality of my experience."

Given the exactitude of anatomy, I wondered if George considered his humanities background a boon or burden. After all, analyzing *Ulysses* had not exactly given me a leg up on memorizing the branches of the facial nerve.

"I feel like my brain is bifurcated, where one half is mushy-gushy feelings and the other half is pathways and chemicals and drugs," George said. "The less I read and the more I study science, the more one predominates. But I never want to lose that humanities aspect. The point is to alleviate suffering at the end of the day."

Yet the rigors of medical school made it all the more difficult for George to keep the humanities in mind:

"A lot of this work requires going numb for hours at a time, to just keep amassing information, like a treadmill that doesn't stop. And in order to do that, emotion has to be removed. It's counterproductive to feel."

After a long night in the library, it was all too easy to forget why we studied, as human beings were reduced to structures, signals and cells. In my sparse clinical encounters, I found it far easier to recall the pathology of disease than the patient's name. I suspected that I, too, was nameless—another furrowed brow, quivering pencil and starched white coat. For George, the only way to avoid losing empathy was to focus, in every encounter, on the patient—to "only connect," as E. M. Forster writes in *Howard's End*. "Only connect the prose and the passion, and both will be exalted, and human love will be seen at its height. Live in fragments no longer."

As medical students, we struggle to connect physician to patient, science to medicine, and medicine to healing. What Forster so readily commands is, in fact, a lifelong pursuit.

"People are more than billions of cells and squishy jelly. It's so easy to dehumanize people in this profession," George admitted. "I'm learning about a protein in one aspect of a disease, and I'm only focused on the protein. You get down to so much detail that the bigger picture of the person is lost—until you go to a clinic and see a person. A full person—with all of their complexity and their beauty."

Only then do both physician and patient become human once more.

My classmates and I each saw a handful of patients in our first year of medical school. Our activities were limited to observing and practicing basic skills; we did not participate directly in patient care. The moment of connection that George and I envision is an idealized interaction, which may be neither representative nor readily obtainable given the brisk encounters and physical demands of medicine, but nonetheless sustains us, just as we are sustained by the experiences that brought us to medicine in the first place: a blot on an MRI, a summer in Ethiopia, a thirst for justice in a world of indifference. Immersed in my own narrative, I feared that, compared to those around me, my own motives for pursuing medicine would seem unconvincing. I did not have a good story to tell.

But did I have good reasons in the first place? Surely there are bad ones, greed and blind ambition among them. But among the varied paths taken by others, I was relieved to discover that my story was as good as any. Only time will tell. For until we become physicians we are students and, as students, we are shadows, each with our own conception of what perfection in this profession entails. We watch and wait, learn and absorb, all the while dreaming of the forms we will take when we come into the light: flawed and beautifully human.

This groundbreaking book by the president and CEO of the Institute for Leadership Education Advancement and Development (I-LEAD) promises to transform thinking within organizations and communities about the fundamental skills required for human progress. David Castro explores the evolution of leadership skills within effective organizations, recognizing that leadership processes have been evolving into different and more promising practices. To capture this trend, David introduces a new concept and a new word, genership, which describes the skill set required for the practice of creativity in groups.

*Better to Speak of It* is a book of core management and personal values written by Robert Rimm, managing editor of Arch Street Press, in collaboration with Clive Gillinson, executive and artistic director of Carnegie Hall. *Better to Speak of It* offers specific, first-hand experiences from many leaders within key nonprofit, corporate, educational and cultural fields, appealing to readers—including nonprofit directors and managers, corporate executives and employees, arts-administration staff and students, and the public interested in the health and well-being of the arts—seeking insight into how creativity can be applied with substantial results.

*Queen of Angels* contrasts Shakespeare with gritty and profane 1970s New York, exploring themes of love, sex, violence, death, faith and coming of age: "These violent delights have violent ends." The novel captures the angst of teenage love striving for maturity within the context of a high-school production of *Romeo and Juliet*, crossing the precarious border between flesh and fantasy that author David Castro—former Philadelphia chief assistant district attorney and now CEO of the Institute for Leadership, Education, Advancement and Development—experienced and observed as a Brooklyn teenager.

Lera Auerbach is a Russian-American poet, composer, musician and visual artist. She has published more than 100 works for opera, ballet, orchestral and chamber music, and performs as a concert pianist throughout the world. Her work is championed by today's leading artists, conductors, stage directors and choreographers. The World Economic Forum in Switzerland selected Lera as a Young Global Leader and then Cultural Leader, where she lectured on borderless creativity. In *Excess of Being*, she revitalizes the form of aphorisms with provocative, dark, ironic and humorous writing that perceptively deals with life's kaleidoscopic questions.

www.ingramcontent.com/pod-product-compliance
Lightning Source LLC
Chambersburg PA
CBHW080508030726
47592CB00011B/3291